bindi
Wildlife Adventures

BOOK
7

CROC
CAPERS

bindi
Wildlife Adventures

CROC
CAPERS

Bindi Irwin
with Chris Kunz

sourcebooks
jabberwocky

Published by Sourcebooks Jabberwocky, an imprint of Sourcebooks, Inc.
P.O. Box 4410, Naperville, Illinois 60567-4410
(630) 961-3900
Fax: (630) 961-2168
www.jabberwockykids.com

First published by Random House Australia in 2010.

Library of Congress Cataloging-in-Publication data is on file with the publisher.

Source of Production: Versa Press, East Peoria, Illinois, USA
Date of Production: June 2012
Run Number: 18001

Printed and bound in the United States of America.
VP 10 9 8 7 6 5 4 3 2 1

*"Only when the last tree has
died and the last river has
been poisoned and the last fish
been caught will we realize we
cannot eat money."*

Cree Indian saying

Dear Diary,

One of my favorite places in the world is the Steve Irwin Wildlife Reserve, named after my dad. We go up to the Cape York Peninsula once a year and take part in estuarine crocodile research.

   This year, Robert and I found some unexpected visitors camping nearby, and we didn't need to dig deep to find out what they were really after. Let me tell you, it certainly wasn't anything to do with appreciating the beautiful wildlife or the stunning Wenlock River!

   It was up to Robert and me to make sure they knew who, and what, they were messing with.

Bindi

CHAPTER ONE

Bindi and Robert Irwin tiptoed through the bushland.

"Was that…?" asked Robert, looking up at a nearby stringybark tree.

"Shhhh!" replied Bindi.

Way off in the distance, an unusual drumming sound could be heard.

"We're getting closer," whispered Bindi, and brother and sister continued tracking the noise.

The Steve Irwin Wildlife Reserve first thing in the morning was a hive of activity. Cockatoos were squawking, lizards were scuttling, and crocs were lurking in the nearby waters of the Wenlock River. Having been woken by the pre-dawn chorus of birds, the siblings were now stalking the elusive palm cockatoo, a beautiful coal-black cockatoo with a large floppy crest and shiny red cheeks that looked like they'd been painted on by an overexcited three-year-old.

Finally the duo found the source of the repetitive drumming. It was a remarkable sight. The cheeky palm cockatoo was holding on to a stick with his claw and banging it against a tree branch, deep in concentration.

Robert was amazed. "I thought you were making it up, Bindi!" he said.

"If you ever need a drummer for your bush band, little buddy, now you know who to ask." She smiled.

"But why do they do it?" asked Robert.

"It's to sound out their territory. He's telling the other birds that this is where he lives and not to take him on."

"Cool," said Robert.

"Super cool," agreed Bindi.

A second later the drumming stopped. A flock of nearby cockatoos squawked loudly and rose like an angry cloud into the clear blue sky. The trill of a great bowerbird could be heard, sounding as though he was complaining about his noisy neighbors.

"Something's got the birds annoyed," said Robert.

Bindi was looking in the direction of the dirt track. "I think I can hear a four-wheel drive coming."

"We weren't expecting any more of the croc-tagging team today, were we?" asked Robert.

"Don't think so," replied Bindi.

Each year the siblings and a team of expert crocodile handlers visited the Steve Irwin Wildlife Reserve to conduct research into crocodile behavior. The Cape York Peninsula was crocodile heaven, and the kids thought it was a pretty perfect place to be as well. This was their favorite classroom in the world, and they loved being able to sit outdoors under towering eucalypts, watching the Australian bush put on its daily performance.

This was remote country—the nearest town, Weipa, was over 50 miles of rough terrain away, so it was unusual to get visitors just dropping in.

"Should we hang around and say

g'day?" asked Robert. "It doesn't sound like the ranger's truck."

Bindi looked at her brother, feeling unsettled. "I wonder who it could be."

The cockatoos still hadn't returned to their gum trees.

"I reckon we should blend into the bush and see who these fellas are," suggested Robert.

Bindi smiled. "You're on. First one up the tree's the winner."

The kids raced off to find the perfect tree to climb…although neither could shake the feeling that this unexpected visitor may not be welcome here.

CHAPTER TWO

Doug and Alice Collins were not happy. The father and daughter were used to air-conditioned rooms, fluffy pillows, and surround-sound home entertainment systems. Yet here they were in the middle of the Australian bush, with camping equipment and little else to keep them entertained.

"Why is Grandpa doing this to you, Dad?" asked eleven-year-old Alice. "And why was I roped into being here too?!"

Doug swatted at a fly buzzing around his face. "You're here because your mother thought that spending quality time with me would stop you from misbehaving at school."

"I didn't do anything wrong. I already told you. I was only defending my right to free speech. Theresa tripping over her desk had nothing to do with me."

Doug sighed. "Look, I don't know

what happened, and frankly I don't care. All I know is that…"

"What do you mean you don't care?" Alice cried. "Your one and only daughter has been accused of something she hasn't done. Why don't you ever stand up for me?"

"Look, darling, work has been flat out at the moment, and I've…"

"Work's always flat out, Dad. It's not fair!"

"Oh, come on, stop the melodrama. We have to make the most of a bad situation."

"At least we agree on one thing. This is definitely a bad situation!" replied Alice haughtily.

The Collinses looked around at what the Irwins had admired only moments before, but they didn't see the same beauty. They saw dirt, leaves, ants, and thousands of other creepy-crawlies.

Doug grumbled under his breath. "This might just be the longest three days of my life."

Alice turned on him. "I heard that!"

They began their attempt to set up their tent. Tent stakes were lost, tent ropes mysteriously became knotted, and, when they finally got the tent up, a small goanna ran under the front flap, prompting an unholy shriek from Alice.

From their perch a short distance away, Bindi and Robert had seen enough. They slid down the trunk of the gum and walked back to their own campsite.

"How can they not see that they're in one of the most beautiful places in the world, Robert?" asked Bindi quietly.

"I don't know, but if we have to spend too much time listening to the two of them bicker, it might be the longest three days of our lives too!"

The brother and sister giggled and happily trotted back to their camp.

CHAPTER THREE

Later that morning, Bindi and Robert were with their mother, Terri, on the banks of the Wenlock River. A couple of members of the croc-tagging team had checked the traps first thing in the morning, and had reported back that they'd caught a croc. The team was now getting ready to get it out of the trap so they could insert the tracking device.

"It looks like a big one, Mum," said Robert.

Terri looked over at the croc. "Yep, I'd say he's around 15 feet long and weighs maybe 1,000 pounds."

Robert's eyes grew big.

Terri smiled at her son. "Nothing we can't handle, Robert. But we'll need all hands on deck for this bloke. Are you up for the job?"

Robert beamed. "Of course."

"Me too, Mum," piped up Bindi.

"Excellent," said Terri, giving both her kids a squeeze. "Let's get to work then."

"Right, gang," said Brad, the man in charge of the croc jump. "Listen up. Once Luke and I release the croc from the trap, you know what to do."

The crew nodded. It wasn't long before they had a rope tied securely around the croc's jaws. Then they jumped onto the croc's back, holding it down. Four large men and Terri, Bindi, and Robert all took part, using their weight to keep the animal still—and getting themselves covered in mud in the process.

It was hot, strenuous work for everyone involved. Although they looked like they could withstand anything, crocodiles did not react well to any sort of tranquilizers. So instead of sedation, brute strength was required to subdue and tag these animals.

Once the animal had quieted down, Dr. Waverley, the scientist who was doing the research into crocodile movements and behaviors, made a small incision in the croc's side and inserted an acoustic tracking device. This was done as quickly and as painlessly as possible. The device would allow Dr. Waverley and his fellow scientists to see the movements of the croc—how far it traveled and when. The team had also set up acoustic receivers along the river, which reported back when the tagged crocs passed by. Because they were such feared creatures, not a lot of research had been done on crocs before Bindi and Robert's father, Steve, came along and showed the world that although some people were scared of crocodiles, they should be as respected and treasured as any other animal. There was still a *lot* to learn about crocs.

Once the reptile had been tagged, they released it back into the river.

"See ya later, alligator," called out Robert.

Everyone winced. In a group of crocodile specialists, calling a crocodile an alligator just wasn't done…unless you were Robert, and you knew it drove everyone crazy!

On the way back to camp, one of the croc handlers, Luke, was chatting to Terri. "So I've set another three floating traps further up the river, and I'm hoping—aggghhh, woo-ouch!" Luke crumpled in a heap.

Bindi rushed toward him. "What's wrong, Luke?"

Luke was doubled over, holding on to his ankle. "Wooouch!" he said again.

Robert couldn't help himself. "What do you mean, *wooouch*?"

Luke groaned. "I think I meant

wow and ouch and the words came out at the same time," he mumbled.

Robert grinned. "Wooouch. Great word. But are you okay?"

Luke finally started using words that people were more familiar with. "I think I've twisted my ankle. That rock there"—he pointed accusingly to a jagged stone nearby. "Didn't see it." He grimaced as he tried to flex his foot.

"Don't put any pressure on it, Luke," said Bindi, getting into nurse mode. "We can help you get back to camp. There's a first-aid kit there."

Luke was grateful. "Thanks, Bindi. I'll be fine, but I don't think

I'll be up to jumping any more crocs until this gets better."

Terri patted him on the shoulder. "No worries, Luke. You just look after yourself."

Robert sniggered. "Might be best if you say a ferocious croc grabbed your ankle as you were wrestling it to the ground," he suggested. "Sounds better than 'I tripped on a rock and twisted my ankle,' doncha think?"

Luke looked over at Robert, wryly. "Yeah, thanks, little mate. I might just do that." Although he knew the injury wasn't serious, Luke was worried about not being able to help out with the croc tagging.

It was risky work with everyone involved. His silly injury was now putting the rest of the team in even more danger!

CHAPTER FOUR

While Terri and Brad took Luke to
the nearest town to confirm that his
sprain was not a break, the kids had
some time off to explore. Robert
wanted to look for a frill-necked
lizard he'd seen nosing around the
campsite the previous afternoon, and

Bindi was happy to come along for the adventure. She knew her brother had a sixth sense when it came to reptiles. He could find lizards anywhere at any time.

They were following tracks in companionable silence when they heard a foreign sound—a sort of gasping noise.

Robert and Bindi looked at each other. They couldn't for the life of them work out what sort of creature made a noise like that. They moved closer to the sound.

Gasp, gasp.

They realized the sound was coming from behind a large bloodwood tree.

They both tiptoed around the base of the tree and…

"Aggggh!" screamed the creature they were stalking. Alice Collins had been quietly sobbing, and now, after that bloodcurdling scream, she began hiccupping. The Irwins weren't sure what to do.

"Sorry—*hiccup*," said Alice, trying to pull herself together. "You scar-*hiccup*-ed me," she explained.

Bindi smiled tentatively. "Don't worry, you sort of scared us too," she replied.

Alice wiped her eyes. "Did you think I sounded like some kind of wild—*hiccup*—creature?" she asked.

27

Robert nodded seriously. "Yeah, we thought we were tracking some new kind of burping goanna or something."

Alice screwed up her face. "Eww, don't mention goannas. They're horrible creatures."

Robert frowned and was about to protest, but Bindi put her hand on his shoulder to quiet him.

"Are you lost?" asked Bindi.

"No, I just had a fight with my dad and wanted some time away from him."

Bindi looked concerned. "If you're not used to the area, it's probably not great for you to just go walking around by yourself," she suggested.

Robert was still annoyed about the girl's anti-lizard comment, and couldn't help adding, "Yeah, there are plenty of really hungry six-foot crocodiles roaming the area, you know."

Alice's eyes got as big as saucers and she jumped to her feet. "What?!"

Bindi shot a disapproving glance at Robert. "They're not roaming around here. But there certainly are estuarine crocodiles in the Wenlock River, not far from here."

"Just when I thought this camping trip couldn't get any worse! I didn't know Grandpa had dropped us off in a crocodile-infested area!"

Bindi could sense the girl was in

danger of becoming hysterical. "We can help you get back to your campsite if you like. I'm Bindi, and this is my brother, Robert."

The girl took a few deep breaths. "Thanks, that would be great," she said. "My name's Alice Collins."

The three kids began walking in the direction of Alice's campsite.

"So, are you on a family camping trip?" asked Bindi, trying to make conversation and cover the fact that Robert was stomping along, still frowning at Alice. Who knew if he'd ever forgive her for the goanna comment.

"Sort of. But it's already a disaster. Grandpa gave Dad this little compass on a silver chain, and it's gone miss-ing since we've arrived here. So Dad immediately blames me, saying I've stolen it. As if! I don't want some stupid old compass anyway. He only notices me when he thinks I've done something wrong. I'm just some sort of nuisance to him, like a buzzing fly that he'd rather swat away than pay attention to…"

"Ohhh, that doesn't sound fair," said Bindi, trying to be supportive. She needn't have bothered, as Alice continued with her tirade.

"It's not even a vacation; it's a work trip. Dad owns a mining com-pany with my grandpa, and there's some mineral or something that he wants to mine here. Grandpa said that rather than spending all his time in an office filling out spreadsheets, Dad should come and check out the land he's planning on mining," said Alice matter-of-factly. "Don't see why he should bother, though; there's nothing much to see."

This was more than Robert could take. He'd been brought up to be polite and well mannered, but this girl was just too much. He let out a war cry—"Whhhhoooooooaaaah!"— and sprinted off into the distance. He didn't want to be around this Alice Collins a moment longer.

Alice looked at Bindi. "What's wrong with your brother?"

Bindi was speechless. There was no way on earth anyone was going to mine the land named after her father! She was going to have to stop this man and his mining company before they even started. She just had to work out how!

CHAPTER FIVE

When the two girls reached the camp site, Bindi wanted to say good-bye to Alice and find somewhere quiet to think through this terrible mining situation, but Alice asked her to stay and meet her father.

Doug Collins was sitting on a fold-up chair outside the tent opening. He was pointing his mobile phone in different directions. "Great, no coverage. How am I supposed to get any work done?"

Alice rolled her eyes. "Dad, I'm back, and I brought a friend with me."

Doug looked up vaguely. "Oh, that's nice. Hello," he said, before concentrating once again on his mobile.

"You need a satellite phone here," said Bindi.

"Of course." Grumbling, he cast the phone aside and brought out some maps. "Finding these mineral springs would have been much easier with the compass your grandpa gave me," Doug said pointedly to Alice.

"I told you, I didn't take the compass," said Alice. "Last time I saw it, it was on the card table there, and then it was gone."

"Things don't just disappear into thin air, Alice," said Doug sternly. "I'm going to take a look at these springs," he said. "Do you want to come along for the walk?"

Alice looked at Bindi. "Um, no thanks. I might stay here with Bindi."

"Okay, then," he said. He gathered up his maps, a hat, and a bottle of water. "I shouldn't be too long. Just need to get an idea of the area, and to work out where the best entry point is to bring in the equipment. See you kids later," he said, and wandered off.

Bindi realized Alice wasn't exaggerating when she mentioned her father's attitude. He really didn't seem to pay much attention to Alice at all! She scowled after him.

Even more importantly, from her point of view, there would be *no* mining equipment coming here. Crocodiles would grow wings and fly backward before that happened!

Alice looked at Bindi, noticing her grim expression. "Hey, Bindi, are you okay?"

Bindi tried to lighten up. "Sure am. I think I might know what happened to your dad's compass," she said.

"Really?" asked Alice.

Bindi smiled. "Let's set up a little experiment." She pointed to a pretty silver chain Alice wore around her neck. "Can you take your necklace off and put it on the card table?" said Bindi.

Alice looked interested. "Okay. Is this a magic trick or something?"

Bindi shook her head. "You said before there was nothing around here. That's not true. The wildlife in this area is extraordinary. There are types of fish and lizards and

39

birds you don't see anywhere else in Australia."

Alice was surprised. "Oh, I just thought it was like every other piece of Australian bush."

"No, it's not. The Steve Irwin Wildlife Reserve has over thirty-five separate ecologies within it."

"What does that mean?" asked Alice, interested.

"It means there are different areas, such as wetlands, rainforests, and bauxite springs, that all have their own set of wildlife, both plants and animals, that make it individual and incredible. And what I'm about to show you," she added, as she

moved the card table with the necklace on it away from the tent and out
into the open, "is one of the things
that makes this area so special."

The girls positioned themselves
a short distance away from the card
table and waited. When Alice started
to talk, Bindi shushed her. After a
while, Bindi climbed a nearby tree.
Alice followed a little nervously,
fumbling as she climbed, and gave a
relieved sigh as she positioned herself on a large branch. "It's quite
comfortable up here," she said, surprised. "It makes the landscape look
more…interesting."

Bindi put her finger to her lips

and pointed. A flash of brown, pink, and gray flew past them, circled the area, and disappeared from sight.

"Wow, what was that?"

"*That* was the great bowerbird," replied Bindi. "And if we stay quiet, I think he'll come back."

They were interrupted by the sound of human whistling. Doug Collins appeared, looking almost relaxed.

"Alice?" he called out.

"Dad, be quiet and stay really still," whispered Alice from the branch.

Doug caught sight of his daughter up a tree, frowned, but kept quiet. He found a trunk to lean against and stood still.

A moment later a loud hissing squawk broke the stillness of the air, and the bowerbird made another loop of the campsite area before landing on the card table.

Father and daughter were entranced.

After glancing around, the bowerbird picked up the necklace with its beak, took off, and headed back into the bush with one last triumphant squawk!

Bindi and Alice climbed down the tree and walked over to Doug.

"So," said Bindi. "There's your thief."

Doug shook his head in disbelief.

CHAPTER SIX

Doug shuffled his feet. "Ahh, sorry for, ahh, accusing you of the theft, Alice," he said, looking completely uncomfortable. Apologies obviously did not come easily to Doug Collins. "Errr, I hope that necklace wasn't valuable," he said, frowning.

"No, it wasn't, Dad," Alice replied. "How fantastic was the bowerbird? I loved the pink feathers on his head. Do you think he saw my silver chain as a gift for him?"

Bindi smiled. "Maybe. It's just like when you stay at someone's house, you come with a present."

Doug cleared his throat. "I need to get back to work." He gathered up his maps and water, and headed back to the chair by the tent.

Alice turned to Bindi. "I'm sorry about my dad, Bindi," she said. "He doesn't even realize he's being rude. He's not used to listening to people. He normally just barks orders."

At that moment, a cry went out. "Bi-indi!"

"Over here, Robert," responded Bindi.

Robert appeared and ran over to her, glaring at Alice on the way. He moved Bindi out of Alice's hearing and whispered to his sister.

Alice watched as Bindi whispered back. Robert frowned. Bindi whispered some more. Robert frowned some more and then nodded.

They returned to Alice. "Sorry about that," said Bindi. "Robert's found something super special that he wants to show me, and I reckon we should show you…and your dad too."

Alice looked delighted. "Really? I'd love that. I'll go and ask Dad." She raced back to the campsite.

Robert looked at Bindi. "Is this a good idea, B?"

Bindi looked fierce. "That man needs to understand exactly what he'll be destroying if he goes ahead with his plans!"

Robert nodded. "It's worth a try."

Alice returned a few moments later with her dad, who looked reluctant.

"How long will this little 'expedition' take?" he asked unenthusiastically.

Bindi answered. "Not long."

"And whereabouts are we heading?" he asked.

"Follow me, and you'll find out," said Robert.

Along the way Bindi pointed out a small cluster of pitcher plants, which, she explained, were an endangered carnivorous plant that attracted insects. When the insects flew or crawled down toward the sweet-smelling liquid at the bottom of the plant, the "lid" would close and the insect would be trapped.

The further they traveled, the more relaxed Doug became. He was starting to look like he might even be enjoying himself. "Are we getting closer to the river?"

Robert nodded. "Yeah, we are."

Alice looked alarmed. "Closer to the river where the crocodiles are?"

Robert nodded again. "Yeah."

"Bindi, is this safe?" Alice asked her friend.

"Well, you always have to be incredibly careful around areas with crocs in them, but we're not going to the water's edge, which would definitely be dangerous. Crocodiles are ambush predators and will lurk in murky water, waiting for the right moment to strike."

The blood was draining from Alice's face. "Ummm, I don't want to get any closer to the riverbank."

Doug looked excited. "I've always

admired the crocodile. Did you know they're the closest living relative to the prehistoric dinosaurs?"

Bindi and Robert laughed. "Yes, we know." They stole a quick glance at one another. So Doug liked crocodiles. This was the first bit of good news they'd had for a while!

Alice was still looking nervous. Doug gave his daughter a quick hug. "Don't worry, honey. If anything acts like it wants to eat you, I'll protect you."

Alice smiled. A hug from her dad. That felt good.

"Almost there," announced Robert,

and he moved off the track a little way to a large mound of vegetation. "Don't make a sound," he said, and the others clambered around.

There in the mound were about 40 eggs, each around 3 inches in length. Little squeaks were coming from the eggs, as if the creatures inside were talking to one another. It was quite extraordinary to hear. The group stayed motionless, listening to the squeaking for a few minutes before Bindi lifted her head, as if sensing something. She whispered, "Guys, I think we need to move away from here now."

As they moved back to the track,

Robert picked up the pair of binoculars from around his neck. "Did you
hear the mum?" he asked Bindi.

"Think so," Bindi replied.

"What sort of bird makes a nest
like that?" asked Alice, looking at
the sky for signs of the mother.

"It's not a bird's nest," said Robert,
looking through the binoculars.

"Is it a turtle's nest?" asked Doug.

"Oh, I love turtles. They're so
cute!" said Alice.

Bindi smiled. "It's not a turtle's
nest," she said.

"Ah, I can see the mother now,"
Robert said, passing the binoculars
to Bindi.

"Yes, she's definitely going toward the nest," confirmed Bindi.

Alice was excited. "Can I have a look too?" she asked, and Bindi handed her the binoculars.

Alice scanned the area. "I can't see anything...Oh, hang on, just a...oh my gosh, oh no, I can see...oh no, the nest, the babies are going to get eaten by a huge..."

CHAPTER SEVEN

Alice passed the binoculars on to her dad, looking horrified. He quickly found what had scared her.

"Wow, it's a croc. Look at her move," Doug said admiringly.

Alice was surprised. "But Dad, that horrible creature is going to eat the eggs."

Robert shook his head, unimpressed. "You better pass the binoculars back to Alice," he said.

Alice took them back and continued watching. The big mother walked right up to the mound and stopped, listening to the squeaking coming from the nest. She looked around, then lay down between the nest and the river to guard her eggs.

Alice put down the binoculars. "So they're croc eggs?" she said, amazed.

"You bet," said Bindi. "The female croc takes care of her eggs, checking on them regularly. She's a fantastic mother. And once the eggs hatch, she carries her babies in her jaws all the way down to the riverbank, so she can watch out for them."

Alice turned to her father. "I had no idea. I've only ever thought of crocodiles as scary, man-eating predators."

Doug agreed. "This gives you quite a different perspective on these animals, doesn't it?" he said.

Robert added, "They care for their families just like humans look after their families. They're not so different from us, apart from the fact they are cold-blooded and we aren't, and they have a few more teeth than we do." He grinned, baring his teeth.

The other three laughed before

they began the journey back to their campsites.

The following morning, the shout went out that there was another croc caught in the traps. But, of course, they were one man down with poor Luke and his twisted ankle, and this croc was larger than yesterday's catch. Bindi and Robert had a quick conference and decided they could solve the problem.

"Mum, we met some campers

yesterday, and I think the dad, Doug, might be really keen to help out with the croc jump."

"Really?" said Terri. "I didn't know there was anyone else camping around here. Well, honey, that would be great. But you know this kind of job isn't suited to just anyone."

Bindi smiled. "I think he'd be a perfect candidate. Back soon." She and Robert raced over to the Collinses' campsite. There was no movement outside the tent, and from inside was the sound of two people snoring.

Robert grinned. "Can I do my feral pig impression and scare them awake?"

Bindi smiled. "Not this morning, little buddy."

She woke them gently and asked Doug if he could help out with the croc tagging. She saw a glimmer of excitement in his eyes, but then it disappeared.

"I have a lot of work to do today," he said.

"C'mon, Dad, you know you want to," prompted Alice.

"Well...it would be quite an experience. I took a zoology class back in my first year of university. I used to love studying animals."

Alice was surprised. "I didn't know that!"

"No, I'd forgotten it myself. Well, okay then. I can help out, I suppose," he said, and his eyes began to sparkle again.

"Take clothes you don't mind getting covered in mud, Doug," warned Robert.

Doug grinned. "This sort of thing is better than being stuck behind a desk all day, that's for sure."

Ten minutes later, the kids and Doug were heading down to the Wenlock River. Alice was still a little tentative, but Bindi explained that they would be surrounded by professional croc handlers, which cheered her up no end…until father

and daughter both spied the crocodile in the trap. He was furious
at having been caught and was
growling deeply.

Alice gulped.

"We-we have to grab him?" said
Doug, looking terrified.

CHAPTER EIGHT

Terri came over and introduced herself to the new recruit. "Well, it's fantastic you've offered to help out, Doug," she said. "This'll be one of the most extraordinary experiences you'll ever have."

"Yes, well, I was just saying I'd

studied a bit of animal science at university, so…it will be, uh…interesting to do some field work."

"Great. Did my kids explain that we're a man down after an incident yesterday?" asked Terri.

Doug looked alarmed. "Do you mean a croc-related incident? Is he all right? Is this going to be dangerous?"

Terri smiled. "Well, compared to, say, taking your dog for a walk, yes it is. But we're all very experienced with this sort of work. Don't worry, we'll keep you away from the sharp end," she said, chuckling to herself.

Doug was not comforted. He

turned to Bindi. "What happened to the other guy?"

"Sprained ankle—he tripped over a rock," she said.

Doug couldn't tell whether Bindi was telling the truth or trying to make him feel better, but Brad, who was once again in charge of the croc team, called the group together and explained what was going to happen.

They set to work, with Doug watching Brad nervously. Once the croc was removed from the traps, it was all action. Brad yelled instructions and, once the jaws had been roped shut, the team, as one, jumped on the croc. This time Alice's dad was part of the team, alongside Bindi and

Robert, and he landed with a thud on the upper tail of the croc—far away from the croc's jaws! He could feel the extraordinary power of the creature underneath him and realized that Terry was right. This truly was a once-in-a-lifetime experience.

Although Alice knew not to distract the crew or upset the croc, she was still jumping up and down with excitement as she watched her dad help wrestle the croc to stillness.

Dr. Waverley asked her if she wanted to help with inserting the tag. She agreed, hesitantly, and went down close to the croc, staring hard at it for a moment.

"It has quite a beautiful range of colors, doesn't it?" she said. She even got brave enough to give it a quick pat before passing Dr. Waverley the surgical equipment. The tag was inserted, the scientist and Alice moved back, and Brad gave the order to leap off the croc. He skillfully removed the jaw ropes and the crocodile, still emitting deep guttural growls, retreated back to the safety of the water.

"Nice work, team, and special thanks to our newest croc wrangler, Doug," announced Brad. The team gave a cheer. Doug grinned. Alice was so proud of her dad!

CHAPTER NINE

The newest croc handler and his daughter were invited to dinner that evening. The Irwins and the croc team were due to leave the next day. They'd had a very successful trip and decided to celebrate with a big bonfire. The adults and the kids sat around toasting marshmallows and listening to the sounds of the bush. Luke got out a harmonica and played a few tunes, which everyone sang along to.

Robert and Bindi had a quick whispered conference away from the others. "Have we done enough?" asked Robert.

"What do you mean?" asked Bindi.

"Do you reckon Doug is still going to want to mine the area?" he asked worriedly.

They turned to look at Doug, who seemed like a different person from the one they'd seen barking orders at his daughter on day one of the camping trip. He had spent time talking to the croc team, and learning about the area and the work they did here. Alice had been worried he would mention his work, but he'd kept quiet and just listened. He was relaxed and obviously enjoying the company of everyone, including his daughter.

"I don't know," said Bindi grimly.

The kids fell asleep a short distance from the campfire, tucked into their swags. The embers of the bonfire flickered, and the stars shone bright. Alice awoke an hour or so later but kept deadly still. Something was climbing over her swag. A couple of days ago she'd have been screaming and shouting by now, but she slowly opened her eyes to find a blue-tongue lizard wandering across her like she was a rock. She didn't disturb him, and he didn't disturb her; he just continued on his way. Alice sat up and saw a cuscus* in a nearby tree. She waved to it, and it looked like it ducked its head in response before disappearing into the tree.

It felt like magic, but this place

* A cuscus is a small, furry, nocturnal marsupial that lives in the Cape York Peninsula and New Guinea.

72

had completely changed for her. It was now full of beautiful creatures that were just going about their business. When you had the time to stop and look around, there was so much to admire. She was hoping like mad her dad felt the same way because now, like Bindi and Robert, she realized it would be a catastrophe if this area was mined.

CHAPTER TEN

The next morning, while the Irwins were packing up their campsite, the Collinses were doing the same. Alice's grandpa would soon be there to pick them up. Both of them were sorry to go, and Alice was particularly going to miss her new friends. Doug and

Alice had hardly spoken a word to one another when they woke, but they'd had breakfast and packed up in companionable silence, breathing in the spirit of the bush.

When the noisy four-wheel drive screeched to a halt next to the camp site, both Alice and Doug looked disappointed that their trip had come to an end.

Grandpa Collins stuck his head out the driver's side window. "G'day Doug, Alice. Righto. All sorted, are we? What's the timeline? When can we get the equipment in and start mining the area?"

Alice realized she was holding her

breath. She watched her father. After all they'd seen, was he really going to continue with his plans to mine?

"Hi, Dad, yes, all good," Doug said.

Alice couldn't help herself. "What?" she screeched. She couldn't believe it. Was it really going to be business as usual after all?

Doug gave her a quick wink before continuing. "Dad, you were right to send me out on this trip. The place will be a nightmare to mine. Access is limited. No mobile coverage. There are noisy cockatoos, ferocious crocs, inquisitive roos, the place is full of crazy scientists wanting to track reptiles and discover new species of plants and whatnot, all a total mess. I'd strongly recommend we scrap plans to mine the bauxite springs here."

"Is that right, son?" Grandpa Collins raised his eyebrows and stared at his son long and hard. "Well, if you say so," he said, his eyes twinkling. "I might just have scoped out a new location that has plenty of bauxite but is part of an existing mining site, so it'll have much less of an impact on the surrounding area."

Doug was confused. "Sounds perfect, Dad," he said, "but how did you know I'd change my mind?"

Grandpa Collins chuckled. "Because way back in the dark ages I came here camping with my dad, and I know how special this place is. You don't remember, but when you were little, I brought you here too. Now you've brought Alice and I reckon when Alice is a parent, she might want to bring her kids here as well."

Alice nodded enthusiastically. She would absolutely, *positively* be bringing her kids here. No doubt about it!

Grandpa Collins continued. "There was no way I was letting you mine this area. But you're so headstrong,

79

I knew you'd have to experience its magic for yourself."

Doug started laughing. "Well, it certainly worked. Alice and I have had a wonderful time."

They started packing the gear into the four-wheel drive.

Once they were ready to go, Alice asked for her grandpa to drive a bit slower on the way out so she could enjoy the scenery. She was looking out for kangaroos when she saw Robert and Bindi running through the trees.

"Slow down, Grandpa. There are my friends."

Bindi and Robert raced over to

the four-wheel drive, puffing and panting. "We went to your campsite but you'd already left," said Bindi, catching her breath. "We wanted to say good-bye and thanks for your help with the croc tagging and, umm, to ask whether…" She stopped, not knowing how to continue.

Bindi and Robert were desperate to find out whether Doug was still planning to mine the area but didn't know how to ask.

Alice grinned. "Over to you, Dad," she said.

Doug got out of the four-wheel drive and spoke to the kids. "Bindi, Robert, I want to thank you both for opening our eyes to the beauty of this landscape. The company's decided this area is incompatible with our mining strategy."

Robert frowned. "What does that mean in English, Doug?"

Doug laughed. "It means we will not be touching the Steve Irwin Wildlife Reserve, not now and not anytime in the future."

Bindi and Robert were thrilled. "Wooo-hoo!" they both shouted.

The Collinses were about to head off when Bindi remembered something. "Oh, Alice, these are for you," she said, handing over Alice's silver necklace and the compass.

"How did you get these back?" asked Alice, amazed.

"Robert and I found the bowerbird's bower near our camp."

Alice smiled. "Anything's possible in this place, don't you think?"

Bindi grinned. "You bet."

Bindi and Robert waved goodbye and took off into the bush, shrieking with happiness. Mission accomplished!

THE SALTWATER OR
ESTUARINE CROCODILE

🐾 The crocodilian family includes freshwater crocodiles, saltwater or estuarine crocodiles, alligators, caimans, and gharials.

🐾 Freshwater crocodiles have longer and thinner snouts, with a straight jawline, and all their teeth are nearly equal in size, while saltwater crocodiles have a broad, powerful-looking snout and an uneven jawline. Their teeth vary in size with some almost twice the size of others.

- The saltwater or estuarine crocodile is Australia's largest apex predator (a predator at the top of the food chain) and the world's largest reptile.

- It is thought that they live from 70 to 100 years of age.

- The saltwater crocodile is usually found in deep, dark, murky water. It may inhabit fresh or salt water but is most commonly found in the brackish estuary areas of northern Australia. (An estuary is an arm or inlet of the sea.)

- Female saltwater crocs can grow up to 11 1/2 feet in length, while males can reach 20 feet in length and weigh over 2,000 pounds.

THE PALM COCKATOO

👣 The palm cockatoo is Australia's largest cockatoo species and is found only in the Cape York Peninsula and New Guinea.

👣 They need a special mix of woodland and rainforest trees for both food and nesting sites, and stringybark and bloodwood trees are their favored eucalypt nesting species.

- Palm cockatoos have been known to beat a hollow tree with a stick or seed pod to sound out their territory.

- The palm cockatoo has one of the largest bills of any parrot species. This powerful bill enables them to eat very hard nuts and seeds that other species have difficulty accessing.

THE GOANNA

🐾 The goanna is a type of monitor lizard that is most commonly found in Australia. There are more species of goanna in Australia than anywhere else in the world!

🐾 There are about thirty species of goanna. They range in size from the short-tailed monitor, which grows to only about 10 inches, to the Komodo dragon, which can grow up to nine feet in length!

- Goannas eat almost any animal they can fit in their mouths, including insects, snakes, birds, rodents, and other lizards.

- Some goannas live in burrows in the ground but some are comfortable up in trees and others in water. Each goanna species is a bit different.

- Most goannas stand on their back legs and "hug" the other goanna when fighting.

- When a Komodo dragon hunts, it doesn't need to totally overpower its prey. Instead, after biting the prey, it can follow the animal for a day or so when the prey usually becomes weak and easier to catch. This is due to bacteria that lives in the dragon's mouth that causes infection in the blood of the prey.

The adventures continue in

bindi
Wildlife Adventures

BOOK
8

SURFING WITH
TURTLES

Turn the page for a sneak peek!

CHAPTER ONE

With her surfboard under one arm, Bindi stood at the water's edge, watching the waves roll in, one after another, in glassy perfection. She felt a rush of excitement. Here she was in Mexico, at Los Cerritos Beach on the Baja Coast! Bindi and Kelly, her American friend, were about to embark on a week-long surf-ari, heading up the west coast, across the border and into San Diego, California.

"Let's carve it up, dude!" Kelly was already paddling out into the surf.

"Gnarly, dude!" Bindi yelled back, giggling. The friends were having fun trying out their surf lingo!

Bindi paddled after her friend. She could just make out Kelly's spiky blond hair as she disappeared behind a steep feathering wave. Kelly threw herself into everything with enthusiasm, especially when it came to sports.

Once they had fought their way

past the break, the friends sat on their surfboards looking back at the shoreline. It was very relaxing bobbing up and down to the rhythm of the sea. What a view! Los Cerritos was an endless strand of soft golden sand set against a backdrop of palm trees. The rugged desert coastline was breathtaking. It seemed a world away from the Sunshine Coast where Bindi usually surfed.

"Did you see our itinerary?" exclaimed Kelly. "Surfing, surfing, and more surfing. This trip is going to rock!" She loved to surf and couldn't imagine anything better than a week of waves.

"Don't forget scoping out marine life on a belly full of fish tacos!" added Bindi, who liked to get her priorities straight.

"*Muy bien!*" agreed Kelly. Bindi knew this phrase meant "very good" in Spanish. Kelly had been teaching her a few Spanish words that could come in handy for the trip.

This was more than an ordinary surf tour; it was also a marine-life adventure. Kelly shared Bindi's passion for animals and their welfare. Her family lived in Oregon and worked for Wildlife Images, a rehabilitation and education center established to care for injured wildlife.

Bindi's mum, Terri, and her brother, Robert, were spending some time in Oregon helping at the center while the lucky girls got to catch some waves.

"Out the back!" Kelly pointed to a rising swell. "This one's mine!"

Bindi watched as Kelly paddled hard until the swell lifted her board onto the wave. Then she jumped to her feet. Bindi was impressed. "Woohoo!" she cheered on her friend.

It was Bindi's turn next and she didn't have to wait long. A picture-perfect wave came along with her name on it. She rehearsed the steps in her head. Board lined up facing the beach. Check. Now paddle! Check.

Bindi moved her arms through the water as fast as she could to propel the board forward. It was hard work getting up the necessary speed to catch the wave before it passed her by. She felt the board lift and begin to speed up. Time to leap up! She pushed herself up to standing. She was surfing!

But then, too late, she realized her perfect little wave was too steep; the nose of her board buried itself into the wave and she was pitched forward. Wipeout!

Under the water, Bindi could feel the pitching and rolling as the wave passed over her and her leg rope gave a sharp tug to remind her she was still attached to her board. She knew enough not to fight the wave but to wait for it to pass over the top of her.

When she came up for air, Bindi swam the few strokes to her board and climbed back on. She lay still for a minute catching her breath, then began paddling toward the beach, allowing the whitewash to carry her in.

Kelly cheered her on. "Great job, Bindi!"

Bindi looked up, surprised. "But I got smashed!" she said as she stood up in the shallow water and placed her board under her arm.

"Yeah, but you did it with style!" That was Kelly for you—always positive, always on the go.

Bindi now noticed that Kelly was standing with an older man. He had shoulder-length hair pulled back in a ponytail and a weathered face that lit up with his broad smile.

"*Buenos días*, Bindi! I'm Matt, your teacher and guide for the next week." He was wearing a colorful surf shirt and a pair of board shorts. As they shook hands Bindi wondered if he had seen her get dumped by the wave.

Matt gave her a smile. "Cerritos is perfect for beginners. It's got one of the nicest swells in all of Baja and is one of the more forgiving places to get dumped."

Bindi cringed. "You saw?"

Matt laughed. "It's nothing to be ashamed of. You can't learn the language of the ocean unless you let her give you a few lessons first!" He gave her a wink. "The others have arrived so we can get started. Are you ready to go out again?"

The glistening ultramarine blue of the Pacific Ocean beckoned to her. Bindi looked over at Kelly, who was practically jumping up and down in excitement.

The two girls spoke at the same time.

"*Sí!*"

"You bet!"

Matt clapped his hands together with enthusiasm. "Let's go surfing!"

Become a
Wildlife Warrior!

Find out how at
www.wildlifewarriors.org.au

Bindi says: "Don't support
companies that directly damage
the environment or support
activities that destroy habitat."